MISS PERTRENIA'S PERSNICKETY CAT

By E.E.Pritchett, MD
Illustrations by: Jeff Duckworth

Published by:
Change The Narrative Publishers
120 S. 2nd Street, #2
Clarksville, TN 37040
First Printing 2020

Dedicated to:

Tomorrow's Child

Special Thanks to **Niambi Mclaurin, Robin Oliver** and **Pertrenia Pressley**

Miss Pertrenia's persnickety cat
went to church wearing a big purple hat.
She was dressed in orange fur and
had a purse of calico.

She meowed and she purred. Up the aisle she did go

and sat in the very first seat, in the very first row.

And as she sat in her
big purple hat,
she heard a clatter
and clamor and
whisper barks too.

Mr. Dowdy's bulldog shouted, "She can't do that, she can't sit there. This is a church for dogs, and she is a cat!"

Miss Pertrenia's persnickety cat, did not move,
no not one inch, she just smiled and sat in her big purple hat.

The bark of the dogs grew loud and louder
until the windows began to shake and the walls shudder.

And then to the stage came the Preacher's Poodle, who held up a paw to stop all the chatter, and ask the dogs just what was the matter.

The dogs began to bark among themselves "cats are showy","gaudy and oh so ostentatious."
"Their shoes are pointy, clothes are frilly and their hats take-up too many spaces".

Mama Rosa's hound dog spoke for the crowd
and said simply, " Preacher Poodle, cats are not allowed."

The Preacher's Poodle asked,
"who made that rule?"

"Well, it's never been done before"
said Little Lucy's cockapoo.

"No it's never been done before. It would be something new!" said Jamal's Collie.

"Maybe", said Miss Pertrenia's persnickety cat,
speaking for the first time since she sat,
"bring a friend who is different from you."
"Oh yes, let's do" said The Preacher's Poodle.

So from Monday to Saturday, they all tried something new. They barked to neighbors, co-workers and their pup's teachers too.

It felt good to share, to invite all kinds of friends
and hope it turned out just right in the end.

The very next week, all dogs church was a wonderful sight to see. There were dogs and cats, mice and chickens too, a goat and a goldfish to name just a few.

There were barks, meows, clucks, and howls, all types of animals were there, singing their songs and reciting their prayers.

Preacher's Poodle stood up front and smiled a big smile as she looked around, from the front to the back, up one aisle and down, the church was filled with all kinds of beautiful animal sounds.

Preacher's Poodle said, "yes, now I see, this is how it is meant to be.
All of us may look different, and may have different names, but we are all
God's children and He loves us the same."

The End

Book Title: **Miss Pertrenia's Pernickety Cat**
Teach This Book!

Book Summary: Miss Pertrenia's Persnickety cat decides to visit All Souls church and creates quite a stir as a cat has never been seen there before. The church is filled with dogs of all kinds, who are confused, and some even angry to see a big fancy hat, and red high heels in church, on a cat! What will they say? What will they do? How would you feel if it were you?

Teaching this Book
Miss Pertrenia's Persnickety Cat is a fun way of teaching children about physical differences, tolerance, and togetherness.

It provides the following teaching opportunities:

1. Connect text with illustrations

2. Identify same, similar, different

3. Explore concept of inclusion, exclusion, tolerance and acceptance

Theme Focus: Accepting those with differences
Comprehension Focus: Same vs. Similar vs Different
Language focus: Include and Exclude

Other CTN Children's Books
Twinland Series: A He and a She
Just Noah, Just Judah
Welcome to Twinland

Miss Mattie Goes to Vote

Visit **CTNBOOKS**.com to order.

Made in the USA
Middletown, DE
06 October 2021